The Miracle
Maker

Uncovering the Hidden Miracles in
Mentorship

Volume 1

Eric D. Capehart, MBA

Foreword by Tifinie Capehart

Published by All The King's Men Publishing – An imprint of All The King's Men, Inc.

The Miracle Maker: Uncovering the Hidden Miracles in Mentorship

ISBN: 0-692-60772-2

ISBN-13: 978-0-692-60772-5

Printed in the United States of America

Dedication

My dearest dedication for this series goes to my wife Tifinie Capehart. Throughout all of the times I've tried to give up on my personal journey and gotten off course; you have been my constant source of inspiration to get back on track. I'd like to share this dedication with our first child Ava Shree. Ava, I'm dedicating this book to you too because you influenced me to step it up and complete this first volume on the miracles found in Mentorship.

The Miracle Maker

Contents

Foreword

Preface

Introduction

The Miracle Maker

Foreword

MIRACLE

noun

mir·a·cle \ˈmir-i-kəl\

"An extraordinary event manifesting divine intervention in human affairs"

Some would say that they do not believe in miracles as it's defined here. Words like extraordinary and divine imply a lack of human control in a situation or outcome. Some people believe that they are in full control of their fate. I believe, like the author, that there is a higher power at work in the many happenings in our lives.

Some events are truly a miracle. For instance, in 2008, meeting my husband and the author of this book was a miracle. In 2007, when all actions were leading me to Chicago, IL. I accepted an urban planning job in the city of Nashville, TN.

The Miracle Maker

And so my adult life in Nashville began, and in 2008 Eric and I crossed paths.

Eric and I found common interests in community activism and volunteerism. During our early courtship, I learned that Eric was the founder of All the Kings Men, Inc. I was immediately drawn to the organization's mission and Eric's passion for mentorship. Now eight years later, I have served as a volunteer, a staff member, and now a Board Member all while playing the role of wife to the CEO and visionary. I've lived through many of the stories that you are about to read. I've also lived through Eric's experience of running a non-profit. Despite the challenges over the years, the purpose and methods still remain the same — to create miracles through mentorship.

I have come to realize that I, too, am a miracle maker. I am now mentoring a young Latina who works in my office. I also had a mentor early in my career who encouraged me to step out of my comfort zone in Kentucky and pursue my dreams. The miracle here is that mentorship just keeps going. It doesn't stop with a singular relationship. It's a seed that is watered with every mentorship relationship that takes places as the result of another. With this idea, mentorship can truly impact the world, and what a miracle that is!

As you read this book, keep in mind that you can be a miracle maker. Eric leaves us with the Miracle Maker Challenge, encouraging us to Find, Connect, and Commit. The relationship with my mentee is just beginning, and I look forward to uncovering the miracles. As you read The Miracle Maker, I hope that you remain open to the possibility that miracles are real and they happen every day. I further hope that you remain open to the possibility of becoming a miracle maker yourself.

The Miracle Maker

Preface

The Miracle Maker: Uncovering the Hidden Miracles in Mentorship is the first volume in a series created in order to share my memories, thoughts, and reflections from my mentorship experiences. The Miracle Maker moniker came about in 2014 as a result of being selected, in my wife's place, to give a TEDx talk in our Antioch community. Tifinie was so engrossed in her important role doing community outreach for NashvilleNext that she decided to release the spot she had been selected for. So, hey, it kind of worked out because I was excited about the opportunity to possibly be on TED.com.

While deciding on a topic and thinking of new ideas to share about it, I wanted to focus and share on a topic that was "in my lane" so to speak. After talking it over with my wife, we came to the obvious topic--mentorship. Now my challenge was coming up with an idea about mentorship, and then writing a TED-worthy talk about it. After considerable thought and prayer, I landed on the idea that by definition mentorship could be considered a miracle. So I went with that idea: mentorship is a miracle. With my idea in mind, I began reflecting on my mentorship experiences. It didn't take long to realize that I was on to something with this idea. After some basic research it also didn't take long for me to realize that my idea wasn't original. However, that didn't change my decision to talk about it. The title of my talk was "The Miracle of Mentorship." The TEDx stage was my opportunity to tell the world what I thought about mentorship and to spread my belief that in every good mentorship relationship any number of miracles can be found. During the promotion of the TEDx event, the organizers put out a post for my talk titled, "Are You a Miracle Maker?" From then on I just considered myself a miracle maker. That's how it all started.

The Miracle Maker

However, I ended up reluctantly having to remove myself from the lineup of speakers for the TEDx event. Can you believe it? At the time I couldn't focus on writing my talk while at the same time having to write papers for school. I'm currently pursuing an MA in Professional Counseling at Liberty University. The decision was tough because I had already written a good portion of my talk when I decided to decline the opportunity. Furthermore, who turns down the opportunity to give a TEDx talk? Nevertheless, even though I feel like my decision resulted in a missed opportunity, I can still find relief in the fact that this book was borne out of the opportunity.

The Miracle Maker

Introduction

I truly believe that mentorship is a miracle. I also believe that you can become a miracle maker just like I have. As you read about my mentorship experiences, I believe you will be able to relate to the stories while enjoying the quick and easy flow of my style of storytelling. I hope my book can be used as an added component or reference to any new mentor training programs in school settings, colleges and universities, nonprofit, and corporate environments.

The Miracle Maker provides an inside look and personal reflections into the influence and power found in mentorship relationships. In this volume I discuss my ideas about building a new mentorship relationship and the function

of a mentor. I use analogies and metaphors to help readers
conceptualize the role of mentor and to clarify some of the
most pressing questions about mentorship. In the end, I hope
to become a distant mentor to anyone who needs mentoring,
and I hope to inspire people all over the world to start a new
mentorship relationship.

ONE

The Origin of All The King's Men

"Where there is no vision the people perish"-- Proverbs

On June 3, 2007, just 34 days after my 26th birthday, two individuals and I founded the mentorship organization All The King's Men. Here is the story.

A few months before we founded All The King's Men, I made a decision to participate in the inaugural Mr. Tennessee Competition, now known as the Mr. Tennessee Scholarship Competition. Looking back on my decision to enter the competition, I can say that it came at a critical juncture in my life.

When I entered the competition, I was a 25-year-old entrepreneur and graduate student always looking for the next opportunity to earn income. When I heard about the Mr. Tennessee Competition, it seemed like the golden opportunity for me because just a few years earlier, while a student at Tennessee State University, I was the second runner up in the 2003 Mr. TSU Pageant. That particular episode in my life came with its own drama and controversy, but that can wait for another volume. With the chance to win $2,000 and the title of Mr. Tennessee, I thought-- I'm all in!

Leading up to the competition, I remember doing as little as possible to prepare for the show-- even waiting until just two weeks before the competition date to fully commit. My final decision to enter the competition came when Dywuan Brown-- my close friend at the time--called me out of the blue and reminded me that I told him that I was going to compete. Dywuan helped with my Mr. TSU Pageant. He asked, "Are you still doing the Mr. Tennessee Competition?"

Dywuan's question sparked something that led to me committing myself wholeheartedly. I thanked Dywuan for calling me because, as I mentioned before, with two weeks until the date I still wasn't at all committed to doing the competition.

That day on the phone we decided that, as a team, we would compete. Dywuan agreed to be my right hand man and my accountability partner as we embarked on a short course towards the competition date that was just a couple of weeks away.

As we planned our strategy to prepare, Dywuan and I decided that we would meet and practice for the competition at my apartment. I was living alone in a one-bedroom apartment in South Nashville and didn't have any real furniture so my spot was ideal for practice. With the competition being so close, we knew we didn't have time to pull together a large cast of volunteers to help us put on a show similar to what we did for the Mr. TSU Pageant. Instead, we decided to focus on what I felt was the most important category in the show--the question and answer category.

As we prepared for the question-and-answer category in the Mr. Tennessee Competition, Dywuan would ask me all kinds of questions. How would you end world hunger? Who's better Mickey Mouse or Donald Duck? No matter how silly or serious Dywuan's questions were, my job was to have an eloquent and appropriate response. We spent so much time preparing for the question and answer category. That was a lot of fun, but even with all the preparation, there was no way I could be prepared for what would eventually happen the night of the Mr. Tennessee Competition.

The final week before the competition I decided to go on a week-long fast from sun-up until sundown. Never having fasted before, I had no idea of what to expect outside of hunger pangs and low energy. While fasting, I was intentional about asking God for his true purpose in my life. At that point I had already had a successful stint with a lawn business right out of college making nearly $30,000 in a summer and managing to blow every cent! The money wasn't enough for me; I didn't care about the money. I wanted to work for a purpose.

The Miracle Maker

After about three days of fasting, my hunger pangs were somewhat under control and instead of hunger for food I had a strong appetite for God's presence. As my fast went on past the third day, I began to experience the incredible presence of the Spirit of the Almighty God. The presence of God was like a cool drink of water on a hot and steamy summer day in Nashville. Like a warm blanket on a cold winter night in New York City. Sweet and gentle. Loving and kind. My prayers to God turned into encounters with God. This was a time in my life when I discovered an intimate relationship with my Father in Heaven and as each day of my fast passed, I grew closer and closer to God and felt his presence like never before.

In the early morning hours of Wednesday, May 30, 2007, God shared an incredible vision with me. God revealed to me the very purpose that would guide my life forever. Tuesday night before I went to sleep, as I was thinking about the upcoming competition, I began to ask God what I would do if I won. As the two weeks of preparation were coming to an end, I still had no solid plans on what I would do if I were to actually win the competition and become Mr. Tennessee. I practiced so much for the question and answer period that I didn't think of what I would do if I actually won. Just after midnight is when God filled my spirit with the incredible vision of All The King's Men. It was like a dam opened in my spirit and rushing out came a vision for something greater than myself. Standing in the kitchen of my small apartment, I grabbed a paper towel from the rack and a pen from that junk drawer in the kitchen that we all seem to have. The first thing I wrote was All The King's Men. That was it. I wrote nothing more than the words All The King's Men.

After I wrote the words All The King's Men on the napkin, I went to lie in my bed. I had no idea that at the time I was receiving an incredible gift from God. Unbeknownst to me I had just written purpose in my life. As I lay in my bed thinking about what I had written, I began to hear a small voice whispering from my heart like a sweet song. It was so sweet. I continued to hear the words All The King's Men being sung from my heart.

After about 20 minutes had passed, still hearing the sweet words ringing in my spirit, I got up from my bed and went back into the kitchen. On the same napkin I originally wrote the name All The King's Men, I began to write a mission statement for All The King's Men and followed that with a curriculum. Until this moment I had no experience with starting organizations and no experience writing a curriculum.

As I was writing I remember looking at my right hand thinking to myself, "I am not in control of my hand." I felt like I was having an out-of-body experience looking at my hand write out the vision for All The King's Men. That was so cool. As I continued writing, I wasn't thinking about anything that I wrote. It's like my pen was bleeding out evidence of what was in my spirit and when I finished writing I felt a great sense of euphoria. All The King's Men had been revealed to me and the entire vision was now written on a paper towel.

On the counter in my small apartment, written on a paper towel and in red ink was the incredible vision of something greater than myself. I received my mission and what I had been praying for. All The King's Men was something that I had never desired to do, but something I felt was the answer to my prayer for purpose in my life.

Fast forwarding to the Mr. Tennessee Competition, let me just say I didn't win. Like in the Mr. TSU Pageant, I was the Second Runner-Up. I was actually pulling for one of the younger contestants to win it. In fact, a younger guy did win it. I was the oldest of the contestants at age 26. I think the other guys were between the ages of 20-22.

I've only told a few people that I never really cared about winning the Mr. Tennessee Competition after my vision and mission was revealed to me. I was laser focused on bringing All The King's Men into existence. On June 3, 2007, during the competition's oratorical segment, I used the stage to announce that I was founding All The Kings Men. Afterwards people were coming up to me shaking my hand and encouraging me to go forward with my vision. One family member of my favorite pick to win came up to me and said, "If you ever run for office, I'd vote for you." I just smiled and said thank you. Even though I lost the competition, I was more excited about what I was getting ready to do. The day after the competition, Dywuan and I met at his house for our first official All The King's Men meeting. Ironically, Dywuan's roommate at the time, Jamie Jackson, walked in right at the beginning of our meeting. I had known Jamie prior to this day.

Jamie asked us what we were doing and we told her that we were starting a mentorship organization called All The King's Men. She then says "I always wanted to start a nonprofit organization." I countered, "Well, here is your chance." That day Dywuan Brown, Jamie Jackson and I became the founders of All The King's Men.

Reflecting on the whole Mr. Tennessee experience, it is clear to me that my journey was not at all about competing for money and a title, but it was about God putting me in position to live out the purpose intended for my life as a mentor. When we started All The King's Men we didn't have many resources to pull off what we knew we had to do. In fact, we didn't know what to expect when we got started. Now after eight years, we can celebrate the fact that we have mentored more than 500 boys through our organization.

Although Dywuan and Jamie have since moved on to pursue their own life's mission; we can each be proud of the foundation we all laid. When we got started we had nothing more than a vision inspired by God and the name All The King's Men. On day one of our mentorship organization we enrolled 15 high school age boys. At first we only met with the guys for group mentoring sessions after school and only one day a week on Saturday mornings. After two weeks the boys started asking if we could meet more than just once a week. That's when we added Mondays and Wednesdays afterschool along with Saturday morning. On day one of the mentoring sessions I told the boys something that I still tell every new group, "I will be here for you until the end." You might stop coming, but I'll always be here for you." The boys came faithfully. That was the first sign that we were on to something.

At first we measured our success by two things: doing all that we could to help the boys refrain from coming into contact with Juvenile court and doing all we could to make sure they all graduate from high school. From those 15 boys, none had any further contact with Juvenile court after joining and all of them went on to graduate from high school. Some of them went on to college, and some even earned scholarships to play college sports. I will never forget that first group of The King's Men.

Although not a part of the first group of mentees, I sadly share the fact that I've had to bury three of my mentees over the span of my eight years of mentoring male youth. DeMarcus Ellis, Laron Owens and Rashad McIntosh were all struck down much too young. Each time it was the result of gun violence. Neither of them were older than 18 years old.

For me, the hidden miracle in this story is the fact that what started off as a selfish ambition to get money turned out to be a catalyst for identifying my selfless purpose. What can explain this outcome of my selfish desire to win a cash prize? No scientific formula connecting the dots of my ambitions and actions can better explain the outcome so let's just consider it a miracle!

TWO

The Miracle of Mentorship

"There are a lot of people making it through. On the other hand, if you can share your feelings and say some things, it probably is going to help a lot of people."

-Tony Dungy-

Anyone who knows me knows that I'm a huge NFL Fan and knows that football is my sport of choice. When I was 10-years-old, I began playing football for the Sevier Park Panthers in my South Nashville neighborhood. Playing football went down just about every day in my hood, but I wanted to take my neighborhood skills to the next level. In other words, "I was ready to put those pads on!"

On my first day of football practice I really didn't know what position I was going to play. Based on my neighborhood skills I already knew I was fast enough to be a running back and I also knew that I could catch pretty good. I figured I'd play one of those positions. My coaches had other plans. Apparently after observing my body type and athletic ability my coaches decided to put me at cornerback. Of course I wanted to run the ball or be a receiver, but I was content to be playing on a team and in them pads! It didn't take long for me to realize that defense was cool and all, but tackling just wasn't my thing. I had the heart, courage and athletic ability to get the job done but I really wanted to play on offense.

As it turns out, my opportunity to play on the offensive side of the ball came when my coaches let me take a shot at playing running back and receiver one day at practice. Running back was like second nature to me but I was way too far down the depth chart to think of getting playing time. That's when I decided to dedicate myself to being a receiver full time. Unfortunately, I think we had one pass play in the playbook, that we almost never called-but I didn't care. I played my position to the fullest.

The Miracle Maker

Those were the days of my life when almost every kid in my neighborhood was living with a single parent. Even though at the time, I was in a single parent home being raised by my mother, I was still able to find a safe place in sports. Not in the streets or a gang, but in sports. Those were the good old days when I became passionate about being an athlete and passionate about being a football player.

Looking back on my middle childhood years, I attribute some of my cognitive development to the game of football. Not having a male in the home and not being influenced by an 'OG' in the hood, playing football taught me how to take multiple aspects of a situation into account and anticipate my next move. Would you agree that this is what mentorship is about?

Some of us would call this common sense, or street sense. I call it mentoring. Playing football as a youth taught me how to learn a designed play, learn everyone's role, and execute the play within a given timeframe. In my mind, the game of football was a mentor to me, meaning the game in itself was teaching me important lessons that would stay with me for the rest of my life. I actually heard former NFL standout Curtis Martin say the exact same thing about football teaching him about life. In fact, many athletes say sports have taught them about life. Is sports some kind of a covert mentor?

Starting at age 10, I went on the play football at every stage of my childhood through my adolescent years. I played varsity football for three years at John Overton High School in Nashville, TN. My final season playing football came during my senior year in high school playing for Lighthouse Christian School in Nashville. Throughout the span of my playing days-- aside from my family and my brother from another mother Benjamin Johnson--the game of football taught me more about life than anything or anyone. Although my playing days were done a couple of moons ago, the principles of the game have yet to fade away.

The Miracle Maker

In 2008, I read Tony Dungy's memoir *Quiet Strength: The Principles, Practices and Priorities of a Winning Life*. Tony's philosophy was simple--coaches are teachers who put faith and family ahead of football. I agree with Coach Dungy. It's his philosophy that helped him lead his team to Super Bowl 41 and become the first African-American head coach to win the Superbowl.

Before I read *Quiet Strength* I had a limited knowledge of Coach Dungy's life and his story outside of football. I only knew of his coaching tenure with the Tampa Bay Buccaneers and then with the Indianapolis Colts until 2009. One thing I distinctly remember is when Tony's oldest son committed suicide during the 2005 NFL Season. What I witnessed from Tony during the remainder of the season inspired me during my own time of mourning. Just one year prior to Coach Dungy's son—who committed suicide at the age of 18-- my family suffered the devastation of losing one of our loved ones. June 23, 2004, was the day of the tragic car accident that led to the death of my oldest sister, Ky'Andreas. Losing a sibling was tough. Losing a sibling in the tragic way that my other sisters and I experienced was horrific. However, nothing was more terrifying than seeing the pain and suffering the loss caused my mother.

From my experience with seeing my mother lose a child, I tried to imagine how Coach Dungy must've felt. I tried to imagine how he could hold it all together and still be a head coach in the NFL. I tried to imagine how a father dealt with such pain. In the summer of 2006, about eight months after Coach Dungy and his family experienced the most unimaginable of tragedies, he was asked to reflect upon the situation in an interview. This is what he said:

"One thing I've learned from this: I'll bet you I've talked to over 200 people in the same situation," Dungy says. "They're going through the same things; it's just that thousands of people don't know about it. On the one hand, it tells you you're not in this by yourself. There are a lot of people making it through. On the other hand, if you can share your feelings and say some things, it probably is going to help a lot of people."

Coach Dungy sharing his feelings and saying other things about his experience helped me heal from my own pain. Coach Dungy sharing his experience helped me come to terms with my own tragedy. Coach Dungy taught me to live and function in the present even with unimaginable pain. After reading about Tony's pain and learning of his emotions about it, my admiration for Coach was made solid and in 2008 when Dungy's memoir *Quiet Strength* was released and became a New York Time's Best Seller, I decided it was a book I needed to read. Do you believe there is a miracle in mentorship?

After reading *Quiet Strength* I gained insight into Coach Dungy's life and how he overcame challenges and obstacles both on and off the field. I also read about his upbringing and about his family life as a husband. As I read his memoir, I began to notice that Coach Dungy and I had some pretty cool things in common. One obvious similarity is that we both have a fondness to football. Another is that we both are now married to beautiful women!

I was also inspired by the fact that in his playing days, Coach Dungy played defensive back just as I did when I first started playing the game at Sevier Park. In his book, Coach Dungy didn't leave his readers hanging with the typical I love my wife and she's my sweetheart story. He shared important relationship lessons from a spiritual perspective. Reading about Coach Dungy's relationship with his wife, Lauren, inspired me to want to get married to a beautiful woman myself. In fact, Coach Dungy opening up about his relationship with his wife taught me that marriage is not so much about looks and feelings, but its more about love, commitment, responsibility, and other important values. Coach Dungy shared lessons about marriage and family life that I hadn't heard because I was growing up with no father in the home. Growing up, I had no tangible example of what a husband was supposed to do for his family.

Reading *Quiet Strength* during my down time as a valet took me about seven days to finish. Each day I would anticipate opening the book as if I were actually about to sit in a room with Coach Dungy and listen to him talk directly to me. When I finished the book, I felt like I had completed a course in Manhood 101 taught by Tony Dungy. I put the book down with the feeling of …Wow, this guy is awesome! The cherry on top was that Coach Dungy played and coached for the Pittsburgh Steelers--my favorite NFL team.

When I finished reading his book, Tony Dungy became my mentor from afar. My experience with the book and what happened to me as a result of learning the principles, practices, and priorities of a winning life are evidence of a miracle. To date I've never been in the same room with Tony Dungy. No phone call. No communication at all. However, that has no effect on my belief that Coach Dungy is one of my mentors.

With only a distant relationship formed from reading his book and a similar fondness for a game, my life has been edified in such a powerful way that I am a better man and more committed husband. The connection that I feel to Coach Dungy and his family cannot be explained in any other means than by calling it a miracle. Can you see the miracle in mentorship? Without any physical connection to a person, you can still find miracles from their mentorship.

THREE

Will You Mentor Me?

"So many times over the years I've heard, and been asked the question, how do I ask someone to mentor me? I'd like to answer this question as simple as I can — I wouldn't advise you to do it."

-Eric Capehart-

How do you ask someone to be your mentor? There is no definitive answer to this question and you're in good luck because you don't have to ask someone to be your mentor. Here's what I believe.

In most any type of relationship, the steps of find, connect, and commit are essential components. You find someone that interests you, establish a connection, and commit to continuing on with it. Mentorship is no different. Fortunately for both parties in a mentorship relationship, similar to some romantic relationships, mentorship relationships are not always meant to last forever. Knowing that mentorship relationships are not always meant to last forever puts the relationship in proper context to a person's life. However, at the same time, the effects of a good mentorship have the potential to last a lifetime.

My best advice for those looking to find a traditional sense of a mentor is to let your mentor find you. Yes, I know this puts the pressure of the new relationship on the mentor to make a move and you may not get the mentor you want, but trust me, in the end, you'll be able uncover a hidden miracle from genuine mentorship to you. Helpful hint: After you read this book give it to someone who you would like to mentor you and see what happens.

I believe mentors should seek out mentees because mentorship requires leading and guiding. What could be worse than you asking a person who you really admire to be your mentor and for whatever reason they decline? How would you feel? Well, this actually happened to me early in my adulthood and it didn't feel good.

The Miracle Maker

While attending an Urban League Young Professionals networking event, a businessman whose name I do remember and whose face I'll never forget was speaking on the importance of surrounding yourself with the right people in order to help yourself rise to the next level professionally. The speaker was dressed in a nice gray suit, wore a nice watch, had clean shoes, and spoke passionately about the importance of having a mentor. The speaker didn't talk on how to find a mentor. Nobody ever talks on how to find a mentor. I think that's because you're probably not supposed to find a mentor. Your mentor has to find you, right? I think so.

The man continued on about his success and how important a handful of people were to him getting ahead in life. As I sat there in my seat listening to his talk, I began scanning my memory for people that had an influence on my life and my path to become a better person. I couldn't think of one person outside of my family that had a significant influence on my life. I had never had a real mentor.

The Miracle Maker

As soon as his talk was over the speaker took questions. The only thing I was thinking was "this guy would be a great mentor for me." As excited I was about the idea of having him as my mentor; I didn't know how to approach the situation. After listening to the speaker's response to a few of the questions from the audience of about 40 young professionals; I made it up in my mind that I was going to ask him if he would mentor me. Asking this question would be taking a huge step out of my comfort zone because typically when I'm at speaking events I tend to be more of a listener than a talker. I like to spend time processing what was said and then developing thoughts, opinions and ideas from there, but this day was different. I saw an opportunity to have what he had. I saw the opportunity to build one of those important relationships with a mentor that he spoke so passionately about. With a rush of energy--more nervousness than anything--I raised my hand to get the speakers attention. Of course someone else raised their hand at the same time as I did. For some reason my heart was pounding. I was so nervous that I thought it showing. I was ready to forestall my question as long as possible, so I decided to let the other person ask their question before I asked mine. The person must have asked what his favorite color was or something that didn't require much thought from him because before I knew it he was looking and pointing in my direction. What is your question?

I thought I had died of nervousness at that moment. I stood up and introduced myself. I spent a few seconds thanking him for sharing his stories and advice with us. Finally, when I couldn't stall any longer, I was ready to ask this man a question that I knew could go really badly and kind of puts him on the spot. But I asked anyway. I said, "Will you mentor me?"

I just knew my heart was going to explode during the few seconds of the silence that followed my question. With what I thought was a reluctant Yes as his answer, I was resuscitated back to life. He told me to hook up with him and that he would give me his contact information. Now I'm hyped up about having a mentor. From an apparent death due to nervousness, I was back to life with the joy of having a mentor. I'm thinking to myself ok, now that I have mentor I'm about to take it to the next level.

The next morning I emailed my new mentor requesting a day and time for us to meet up and do what I thought of as "mentor stuff." A day or two passed and I hadn't heard back from my mentor. I decided to call the number on his personal business card from the company he started. No answer. I left a message expressing how grateful I was that he decided to mentor me and that I was looking forward to talking with him in the near future. A week passed then two more weeks pass and I still hadn't heard from my new mentor. I decided to reach out to another Urban League Young Professionals member Shawn Thompson to see if he by chance knew how to reach my mentor. Turns out the speaker was the advisor to ULYP so reaching him was not going to be difficult. Shawn had good things to say about this man and told me stories of how he had been helpful in the past. All of it sounded good, but in my mind it wasn't adding up because I was having a different experience. No experience. Shawn encouraged me to keep reaching out to him because he was a busy man. I figured that what Shawn said to me made perfect sense. I reasoned that he's a business man, he has lots of people to talk to and I'm just another person on the list, I'll try to reach him again.

In the end, I spoke with my first mentor only once after meeting him. Our first and last conversation was about as awkward as you can imagine. Remember my analogy about mentor relationships: find, connect and commit. Let's just say that our relationship didn't quite connect. Which goes back to why I cringe when asked the question "How do I ask someone to mentor me?"

Although this quick mentorship relationship may seem unfortunate for me, which is exactly how I initially felt, looking back there is still a miracle to be found from my first "mentor." After all, how could I have ever imagined such a short and seemingly irrelevant mentorship experience would be mentioned in my own book about mentorship? My experience

highlights the lesson of not saying yes when you really mean

maybe or no.

FOUR

Mike and Davontae

"The beginning of a new Mentorship relationship is an incredible moment that marks the start of an odyssey to uncover a hidden miracle."

-Eric Capehart-

Every year at All The King's Men I find myself enrolling any number of new mentees into our organization. Now thinking about it, the beginning of the school year is my official time I call embarking. Embarking is the time when you start your journey to find the miracles in your mentorship. I'd say that the majority of new mentors are not going into the mentorship relationship expecting a miracle. If you're a new mentor or an experienced one, don't forget to embark. Go into the relationship expecting to be a miracle maker.

In 2009, nearing the end of our second year, Dywuan and I were facilitating our group mentorship sessions at Hadley

Park Community Center in Nashville when two young men were referred to us from their basketball coach. Their coach told his team that if they wanted to play for him they had to join All The King's Men. Ironically, we didn't know anything about this coach or his requirement, but that didn't stop us from allowing the two guys that actually showed up from joining our group.

The first day the two came to our session I can remember the older, more vocal and brash Michael Battle bursting into the kitchen where we were making our meal for the session. I'll never forget Michael's six foot muscular frame coming through the door nearly knocking other students out of his way as he made a bee-line towards the food yelling "I'm hungry, where the food at!" At first I laughed because I found humor in Mike's way of introducing himself to our group, then I quickly took control of the situation in a cool respectful way. I'm not one for putting someone on "Front Street", so I handled the situation with ease and care. Plus I had no idea who this man-child was. Then I noticed a smaller framed five-foot-five guy walk in right behind Mike. Davontae Rucker, the smaller guy, walked in and kind of surveyed the kitchen looking for what I assume was a familiar face. Unlike Mike, Davontae didn't make any noise and didn't really say anything at all. I could tell Davontae was the calmer one, but I still didn't know who he was or anything about him. I told both Mike and Davontae that in order to get some of the food we were preparing they had to be members of All The King's Men, and that's when I was made aware of their coaches demands.

When Mike and Davontae came to us, Dywuan and I were already mentoring around 20 boys whose ages ranged from 8 to 17 years old. At first we were a little concerned with how well the two would mesh with the other boys, but in the end we decided to go ahead and let them join. After all, that was what we were there for. That day Mike and Davontae joined All The King's Men, and went on to become the first two lifetime members of our organization. Lifetime membership is awarded to high school graduates who are members of All The King's Men. This is pretty much a small introduction to my mentees Mike and Davontae. Of course there are many stories that fall in between.

Until that fateful day of me meeting Mike and Davontae, I had never thought about being a person's individual mentor. After the planned session on the day that Mike and Davontae came to us, Dywuan and I did what we always did. Dywuan and I had a private sit down with both of the guys to give them an orientation of what All The King's Men was all about. We started off introducing ourselves and letting them know that we were the ones in charge. Soon after our talk, both of the guys began to tell us about them being involved in a police raid of an abandoned property in North Nashville right before they came to the community center that day. They informed us that some of the guys they were with ended up getting arrested, but they didn't. As soon as they were free, they came to the community center and ended up joining

The Miracle Maker

All The King's Men. I don't know why, but for some reason by the end of our time with them that day, Dywuan and I had decided to personally take responsibility for mentoring these two guys one-on-one. Dywuan picked Mike and I took on Davontae. Looking back, I can say that my decision to mentor Davonte was my official embarkment on the journey to discover the miracle of my mentorship to him.

The reason I've shared about Mike and Davontae is to introduce an important part of the mentorship relationship which are the backstories of the individuals involved. These are the stories of the lives of the people involved in the mentor relationship. Over the years, working with and training new mentors, I've learned that no matter what your backstory is, every person (even you) is uniquely qualified to be a great mentor. I believe this because no matter the circumstances of your life, no matter how far down the road in life you are, I can guarantee you that someone, somewhere needs to know the lessons you've learned to help them find inspiration and hope

in their own life.

FIVE

The Backstories

"Somewhere along my journey of life I picked up a valuable lesson that taught me that anytime you want to know why a thing is the way it is, you need to know the history behind that thing."

-Eric Capehart-

I want to introduce an important part of the mentorship relationship which I call the *backstories* of the individuals involved. These are the stories of the lives of the people involved in the mentor relationship. In counseling, there is a theory that refers to life experience as a person's narrative, or a person's story. Narrative therapists believe that a person's life is a compilation of stories that can be used to find meaning from life. Think of the backstory in the same way. Doing so is important because being aware of the backstories lays the foundation for a new story and clears the path towards

uncovering any potential hidden miracles.

When we first started All The King's Men, my

backstory played a critical role in gaining credibility from the

boys we would eventually be mentoring. In 1998, during the

last months of my junior year of high school I was caught red-

handed buying a bag of weed from another student and was

subsequently expelled for a whole calendar year.

While playing sports in high school, and having a job, I

decided that I was going to make more money hustling weed. I

partnered up with my closest high school friend and we started

our own little enterprise. Business was good for us from the

start because we had the plug on the good stuff everybody

wanted plus being a weed smoker myself at the time, I already

knew who our clientele would be. Once word got out that we

had the goods, we quickly gained a considerable market share.

The whole time I was hustling weed I felt that I needed to quit before it was too late. Being young, I didn't think that time would eventually catch up with me. Of course I was wrong.

On the morning of March 30, 1998, a page in my backstory that changed my life forever, I decided that I was no longer going to sell weed at school. My decision was in part because I didn't feel like walking around all day with 7 grams of weed in my shoes under my feet. My partner and I used to move our product by keeping our stash in each of our shoes with hopes of selling out as the school day went on; but this particular morning I wasn't feeling good about walking around with lumps of weed pressing on the soles of my feet all day. Knowing that I didn't have any sales lined up I decided to leave my stash at home.

When I got to school I was kind of feeling good about not having weed in my shoes. I felt free, and like a regular student not having to worry about the consequences of being the 'weed man.' All that quickly went away in the moment when my partner asked me to do him a favor. At the school pep rally that morning, my partner told me that he too had left his stash at home and needed me to serve one of our customers. I told him that I had left my stash at home too, but not to worry because I knew another guy that smoked and always had weed on him. I told my homie that I would pick up the sack on my way to my second period class and that I would make the sale for him because I would see the customer before he would. That was the plan, but that's not what happened.

On my way to my second period class, I stopped and met with the guy I needed to see to get the sack. We had the same second period class so he wasn't hard to find. I told him that all I needed was a gram and we decided to meet in the bathroom to make the deal happen. As we walked into the bathroom I followed him as he walked into the last stall furthest away from the entrance to the bathroom. With my back turned to the bathroom entrance, I took the sack from my classmate. Suddenly we hear a male voice that says, "Give it to me!" As soon as I heard the voice, I noticed the other guy quickly move back into the stall as if he was trying to hide from the teacher that had apparently followed us into the bathroom and watched our transaction. I turned around and handed him the dime bag of weed that ended up costing me a one year suspension from all public schools in Nashville. This was in March at the end of my junior year which meant that I was expelled until April of my senior year. As you can imagine, I had some hard days ahead when I was expelled, but with a lot of help and sacrifice from my mother, and some work of my own, I was able to serve my suspension, return to school, and graduate on time.

Earlier in the book I introduced you to Mike and Davontae. Both of these men are special to me and have interesting backstories. I bring these men up again because one of them has a backstory with an episode similar to my own.

After meeting Davontae Rucker and accepting him as my personal mentee, I began to learn more about his backstory. Ironically, Davontae was a senior in high school that was

41

coming up on the end of his one-year suspension from public schools because he too had been caught in possession of weed. Even though Davontae was expelled from school, he was enrolled in an alternative school for students who had been kicked out of the public schools. When Davontae told me about his situation, I couldn't believe it, and I felt obligated to mentor him. In that moment I was able to find meaning from my own experience of expulsion. My expulsion experience came full circle.

My perspective on Davontae and his situation was that if I could overcome the pitfalls of expulsion from school, graduate on time and go to college-- he could too. There I was in a position to take a negative episode from my backstory and use it as a guide map to help someone else in the same position. Davontae's suspension was set to end a few months after we met. He told me that he wanted to go back to his zoned public school, graduate on time and go to college. Exactly what I did. My conviction to help Davontae get to college was so strong I felt I would be less of a man if I didn't put forth the effort to actually help him. It became clear to me that if I didn't help I was merely a part of the problem.

I decided that I would pick Davontae up from the alternative school every day until his suspension was over. This was necessary because he was finding it hard to stay positive in the negative environment of the alternative school. I figured after school was a good time for him to cool out and release whatever was on his mind. At first he thought I was the police, and that made for some awkward moments. When I asked him why he thought I was the police, he said that he had never met anyone who wanted to help that wasn't up to something dodgy. As it turns out somebody was up to something. Even though we didn't know it, God was up to something.

During our after school conversations, Davontae eventually realized that I wasn't the police. This was critical because as soon as the idea that I was the police was out of the way; trust was established and Davontae opened up to me. He always talked about going to college, as many young people do, but also similar to many young people in his situation, he had no real idea of what it would take to actually make it to college. Along with our talks about college were talks about God and Spirituality. Davontae had lots of questions about God and the Bible. He told me that he wanted to learn more about Spirituality and the Bible. Davontae's interest in God and Spirituality is key here because his life and affiliations wouldn't lead you to think he was at all concerned with matters of God or Spirituality.

Davontae was known in the streets of his hood because he was a well-known member of the Bloods gang. When we met, Tae had already put in enough work to gain a reputation as somebody that wasn't playing no games in the streets. I never saw Davontae as a dangerous gang member, I saw something else. I actually saw myself in Davontae. My perspective of Davontae and his situation is important. I'll speak more on perspective later.

The Miracle Maker

As time went on and Davontae's suspension came to an end, he returned to his public school with a new attitude and a sense of hope for the future. I wish I could say that things were all good from this point on, but that's not how the story goes. Facing a considerable amount of obstacles, Davontae, with guidance from me as his mentor, was able to graduate from high school on time after serving a one-year suspension from public schools. Is this not a miracle of mentorship? Davonte would tell you yes, because not only did he graduate, he also got accepted to and went on to attend Tennessee State University. My alma mater! Another miracle of mentorship!

As the semesters went on at TSU, Davontae was not able to find his place on campus, but not because he couldn't succeed. Davontae wanted more. During his second year of attending TSU Davontae made a decision to leave there to enroll at The Well Discipleship Training School in Atlanta, Ga where he would spend the next 4 years of his journey. While overcoming numerous challenges while at The Well, Davontae is now a Well graduate, a full time missionary, and engaged to be married. While attending The Well, Davontae also enrolled into the Atlanta Metro College where he is now completing his degree in History. I couldn't be more proud of Davontae!

This chapter is all about the backstory and how they are important in uncovering the hidden miracles in mentorship. With my own backstory and Davontae's backstory, which are separated by 10 years, we started a new story with our mentorship relationship. Since the beginning, Davontae and I have discussed numerous miracles found in our mentorship relationship.

At the time when I was being expelled from school I felt as bad as I had ever felt in life, but God knew that years later I would need to take my backstory and use it to help someone get closer to Him. Today Davontae has renounced his gang affiliation, completed his discipleship training, and wrote a book about his experience over a two-year span of his life. Ask him about any of this and Davontae will tell you that these are

the miracles of mentorship.

Reflection

What is your backstory?

SIX

Captain of the Ship

"You don't have to know everything, but you need to know something."

-Eric Capehart-

So many times I hear people say, "I don't know what I have to offer as a mentor." To me this is a self-declaration asserting that even though you've managed to live your life to this point, you don't think you've learned or experienced anything significant enough to actually help someone else. I say show me a person who has lived more than a week and I'll show you someone capable of being mentor.

I understand that the most uncomfortable relationships to start is one that puts all of the onus on a single member of the relationship. But I truly believe accepting this responsibility is what the mentor relationship is all about. As I mentioned before, the first step towards developing the relationship is on the mentor and that's because in a mentor relationship you are the captain of the "ship." As the captain of your mentor-ship, your responsibility is pointing your mentee in the right direction, establishing benchmarks and checkpoints, and guiding your mentee on their path towards whatever the relationship shall bring.

Yes, in the beginning of the mentor relationship it's all about you and not at all about the mentee, but we are only talking about the start of the relationship. Once the relationship is started, and the ship is sailing per se, the responsibility becomes more balanced. The old adage "you can lead a horse to water, but you can't make him drink" sums up my point. Even though your mentee needs to actually drink for themselves, as the adage states the horse needs to be led. Hopefully you're not really mentoring a horse!

Don't feel the pressure to think you have to know what to say all the time and always be right. Keep calm and know that you don't have to know everything, but you need to know something. Whatever your backstory has to offer is what you can speak on, because this is what you know. You're an expert on your life and your backstory. If you believe this, and can accept that the start of the mentor relationship is on you, the mentor, then I believe you are ready to embark on your journey towards becoming a miracle maker.

Aye, aye captain!

The Miracle Maker

SEVEN

Perspective in Mentorship

"...instead of answering the question with instruction you could simply offer different perspectives to consider in the decision making process of your mentee."

-Eric Capehart-

About five months into the pregnancy of our first child, Ava, to whom this book is dedicated, my wife and I decided that we wanted to share the news with our social networks. We decided our upcoming date night at Kevin Hart's 'What Now' Tour would be a fun time to take a few pictures and post them on Facebook to make it "official." We're in an era where a post on Facebook makes something official.

Not to my surprise, our post exploded with comments full of blessings and love. I don't know about my wife, but I was blown away with the outpouring of love and well-wishes from so many people. As I read through each comment I smiled with joy because I actually knew the author of the comments and their words struck me as if they were saying them to us face-to-face. I've got to say it--I'm a low key kind of guy and all the likes and comments kind of overwhelmed my social media attention span. I enjoy social media as much as the next person, but as with everyone else, I use it for how I see fit.

I want to start this discussion on perspective by talking on a subject that we are all familiar with, social media. For instance, my personal Instagram page is solely a place to store my personal picture collection. That's it! That's why I started the account. If you like the pictures-good! The thing is, I love taking pictures and I needed a place to store my coolest pictures and Instagram met my needs. My Facebook account on the other hand is a place for me to post things that I'm interested in at the time or articles I want to share with my network. Twitter is my where I go get information about the things I'm interested in. Along with staying in touch with close friends, distant friends and my family this pretty much sums up my personal use of social media.

I just gave you a glimpse of my perspective or outlook on the use of social media. Each of us has our own perspective on any given number of things. One critical thing to note is that a perspective is not necessarily a fact or truth. You can have your perspective, but remember it's just that, your perspective. For your mentee, sharing your perspective is critical.

Mentorship is about offering a new, and different perspective for your mentee to consider. Mentees ask questions because they want our perspective on their ideas, beliefs, and so on. As a mentor, your job is not to fix anyone's problems, or have all the keys to life's challenges. Instead a good mentor offers a new perspective for the mentee to consider. A new way to view a situation or a decision. One of my mentees Dr. Drake Dudley and I were discussing the concept of perspective and he said, "People pay for perspective E." He's right! I had never heard that before, but I get it. Drake went on to say the reason he asks me questions is because he wants my perspective. Not a solution.

The problem occurs when mentees ask their mentor the wrong question. The "What do you think I should do?" question. Mentors beware of this question! Just because your mentee asks *"what I should do,"* does not mean you need to tell them what they should do. After all, telling someone what to do is not exactly mentoring, it's telling someone what to do. Instead of answering the question with instructions on what to do, you could simply offer different perspectives for your mentee to consider in their decision making process. I think this is a key sign of a good mentor.

Biblical scripture gives a clear example on the power of perspective. In John 5, as Jesus approached the gates near the pool of Bethesda in Jerusalem where the sick and crippled went to be healed, he noticed a man who appeared to have been crippled for a long time. Jesus approached the man and asked him "Do you want to get well?" In answering Jesus' question,

the crippled man laments about how people pass by him daily

offering no help to get to the pool where he can be healed. I

think Jesus' question to the man provides us a glimpse into his

perspective. Imagine if you will for a moment that you are Jesus

and you approached this man, what perspective would you

have?

The man's perspective is clear; everyone else is

responsible for helping him in order for him to help himself.

Clearly, Jesus didn't perceive the man in the way the man

thought of himself. Jesus tells the man "Stand up pick up your

mat and walk" (John 5:8). I'd like to think that the crippled man

took a minute to evaluate what Jesus was telling him to do.

After all, this man had been crippled for so long that perhaps

even the idea of standing up and walking never entered his

mind because he couldn't see himself doing either. When Jesus

asked the man "Do you want to get well?" I think the man

actually viewed his situation from Jesus' perspective and

perhaps for the first time decided that getting up and walking was possible. It didn't take long for the new perspective to kick in with the cripple man because the man jumped up and ran away full of joy and gladness.

Jesus didn't come to the crippled man as a mentor because he had a higher purpose. However, in this story, Jesus gives us an important lesson on having proper perspective as a mentor. Because of Jesus' backstory and his ultimate power, he was able to see the crippled man not for his disability but for his potential. That's what mentors do, we are the more experienced experts on life and because of this will always have a different perspective on the situations our mentees find themselves in. Therefore, like Jesus, mentors need to be ready and able to offer new perspectives for mentees. Jesus could have simply healed the man without asking him anything. Instead Jesus challenged the crippled man to examine his true desires by asking what I call a perspective forming question. A cool thing about questions is that when asked, the receiver's brain can't help but think about it, and answer it. What if I told you that everything you wanted to do, you could?

I like what Jesus does with his use of questioning in this situation. Instead of asking the man, why don't you just get up and walk? Jesus knows that why questions put people in defense mode, so instead of asking a why question, Jesus asks a do you question. Asking do you want to get well gets the man to ask himself a question that at the same time gave him new perspective on his situation.

I hope my message on perspective is clear, but if it's not let me make it clear for you. Don't be that mentor that's always telling your mentee what they need to do. Instead, give them your perspective on the given situation, and let them decide what they'll do for themselves. Hopefully our mentees will always make the decision that leads to happiness. The reason you don't tell mentees what to do is simple; they have to live with the results of the decision, and why would you want your mentee to live out your decision for their life? Resist the urge to tell your mentee what to do, and embrace the idea of sharing

your perspective with your mentee.

EIGHT

Mentorship Only Takes a Moment

"Knowing the value of every moment in your mentorship is your secret weapon."

-Eric Capehart-

My mentor Ron Johnson is a world traveler and professional speaker from Memphis, TN. Ron is better known as "Ronnie Key" to his family, and "Spiderman" to his football teammates at Tennessee State University during the early 80's. Either way, I call him Ron. Meeting Ron is another one of those moments in my backstory that's had a lasting impact. I'll call it a miracle. Since day one of me meeting Ron, who is nearly 20 years older than me, has been consistently in my life as a friend, brother, and a mentor. Through our mentor relationship Ron has taught me an important lesson about the precious moments of life.

The Miracle Maker

Ron is the Director of Reaching Excellence as Leaders program at Nashville's Oasis Center. For 30 years Ron has mentored thousands of young people who have found themselves in trouble with the law or who may need a positive male influence in their lives. Ron is the perfect man for the job he holds because trouble with the law is something he had plenty of experience with.

Listening to his stories of a quick-tempered, pistol-carrying, drug kingpin, growing up in some of the toughest streets in Memphis always puts me on edge. While listening to his stories, I find myself hanging onto every detail of the story thinking to myself at any time in this story everything can go tragically wrong for somebody. Story after story is filled with testimony you wouldn't believe was true if you met Ron today. Of course there is the side of the story that included large amounts of cash, partying, and women. When Ron shares episodes from his backstory they seem so glorious, but that's only one side of the reality.

The Miracle Maker

With all the seriously dangerous moments of Ron's youth and into his early adulthood, one of Ron's biggest lessons learned is that all it takes is a single moment in time for all of life to be altered forever. No moment taught Ron this lesson more than the moment he was informed of his mother's murder during his senior year at Tennessee State University.

Ron's backstory reveals many of the moments that had a profound impact on his life. Eventually spending 3 1/2 years in a federal prison on a 30-year sentence from a drug kingpin charge, Ron considers himself blessed to be alive and free.

One particular moment that Ron likes to share is his vivid memory of a moment from his childhood playing in a sandbox in the middle of the projects he lived in. Ron recalls the moment when two sisters teased him because he believed that one day he would get in a plane and fly all over the world. One day while playing in the projects, Ron pointed towards a plane in the sky and declared his vision for his future. When Ron made his declaration, the two sisters laughed at him because his dream was too far from their reality. I know without a doubt that that moment playing as a child altered his life forever.

Today, in his daily work and as he travels the world as speaker and expert on Delinquency Prevention and Intervention, Ron speaks on the importance of living in the moment. Never neglecting the importance of planning for the future, Ron speaks on being in the now--the single moment that we all share. Any one of Ron's personal stories highlights the importance of a single moment. Just about every time he goes to speak to young people or adults, Ron quotes this poem written by Dr. Benjamin E. Mays titled Just a Minute:

"I have only just a minute, only sixty-seconds in it. Forced upon me, can't refuse it. Didn't seek it, didn't choose it. But it's up to me to use it. I must suffer if I lose it, give an account if I abuse it, a tiny little minute, but eternity is in it."

Knowing the value of every moment in your mentorship is your secret weapon on your journey towards uncovering the miracle in your mentorship. What I love about mentorship is the fact that each moment spent with your mentee holds eternity. To me this means that any given second I spend with any one of my mentees is the most important moment in our relationship. A good example of the importance every minute spent in a mentor relationship is when your mentee reminds you of something you said or did that had a lasting impact on them. When your mentee tells you of something that you said or did that stuck with them, they are referring to a single moment in your mentorship to them. A single moment that held eternity.

The concept of this chapter is easily understood by adults because most of us have learned the value of time and the importance of managing it well. However, for young people this concept is a little harder to grasp and I think it's because when we're young we truly think we have all the time in the world, making it hard to realize the impact of a single moment in time. There are far too many miracles to speak on when thinking about my mentorship from Ron, but learning that life

is all about the present moment is a gem that should be shared

for generations to come.

NINE

My Miracle Maker Challenge

#FindConnectCommit

Do you believe in miracles? Some psychologists believe that there is no such thing as a miracle and that anyone who claims to have experienced a miracle is in fact a delusional person. Well, I guess that means I'm a delusional person! Just kidding, there is nothing delusional about knowing that there are miracles that happen from mentorship relationships. In fact, I believe in the miracle of mentorship so much that I've decided to go on a campaign to encourage every person in the world to consider mentoring someone before their time on this Earth comes to an end. That's 7 billion mentors!

If you've ever had a great mentor I want you to think about how the relationship started, the backstories and then think of the fruits of the relationship. Next, I want you to ask yourself how this could have possibly happened? Was this because of your own doing? Was it just a fluke? Was it real? After thinking on these questions, I believe you'll begin to notice that the relationship is divine coincidence that cannot be explained by any other means than by a miracle.

Before I close this first volume of *The Miracle Maker: Uncovering the Hidden Miracles in Mentorship*, I want to share a final story about the miracle of mentorship. Like I said earlier, every year I personally choose one person who I am going to mentor one-on-one. This all started with Davontae Rucker. Also, as I've said before, I think every person has what it takes to mentor somebody even if they don't think they have anything to offer. If you've lived and learned anything at all from your backstory, then I can almost guarantee you that someone, somewhere is waiting on your mentorship. My wife found this out one day while she was engaged with a co-worker at her job.

As my wife Tifinie was talking with her younger co-worker she was made aware of the influence she was having on this person. This woman, influenced by my wife, is a 20 something year old woman of Hispanic descent. My wife is a 30 something year old woman of African descent. During their conversation, my wife was told that she was already serving as an example to her younger and less experienced co-worker. Tifinie's co-worker told her exactly how she was making a lasting influence on her, pointing to their similarities as minority women working in their field, to professionalism in the office. Being married to me and seeing the impact of my mentorship to hundreds of boys, my wife was happy to learn of the influence she was having on her co-worker.

After their discussion, my wife tells me that she was reminded of my philosophy of choosing your mentee, and not waiting on them to ask for your mentorship. Right then, my wife decided to become a miracle maker. She decided that she was going to be her younger co-workers mentor. That day my wife became a miracle maker because she gave her intentional mentorship to her younger co-worker. My wife told her younger co-worker that she wanted to be her mentor and that's when her co-worker told her that she already was her mentor in her eyes. Is this not a miracle? Now, with my wife's new awareness of her influence, their two backstories have collided and they have started a journey towards finding any hidden miracles in mentorship. Now my wife is always eager to tell me about the time she spends with her mentee.

So who will your next mentee be? Maybe it's the person who makes your coffee at Starbucks every day that is waiting on your mentorship. Perhaps the person waiting on your mentorship is a student in your class or, like my wife, maybe it's your co-worker. Maybe, just maybe, your new mentee is a person who you see every day in passing and notice along the way. I don't know who your next mentee is going to be, but what I do know is that if you take these three easy steps you can become a miracle maker.

Find, connect, commit. These are the three steps towards starting a new mentor relationship. I've made it clear that I believe asking someone to mentor you isn't necessary, and you shouldn't do it. At the same time if you ask someone to mentor you and they accept your invitation — good for you. I hope things work out and you get what you're looking for. In the case they decline, or accept you but fail to be a good mentor, you can still use that person as your mentor as I do with Tony Dungy. The point here is that I'm challenging you to become a mentor to somebody. I know this is no easy task for new mentors, but I hope my easy formula is a start.

Over the next 30 days I want you to begin to be intentional about mentoring somebody. Let me break the steps down for you. Note that even in the case when you're mentoring with an established mentorship organization- you can still be a miracle maker!

Step one is finding a mentee. You can find this person by knocking. Here is how you knock. Pay attention to people that you may see something in that they may not see in themselves. Careful observation is the key here, don't just randomly pick someone. Narrow your search down to 1 to 3 people and begin talking with each person about what you see in them. Knocking is all about starting a conversation with your mentee recruit. You can let them know that you've noticed something in them and want to learn more about their goals or plans for the future. This is when you need to pay close attention to their backstory. In fact- you need to ask for the backstory. You can use this question; tell me something about you that I wouldn't know unless you told me? While listening to their backstory, listen for clues to inform you on if this is the right person for you to mentor. In my opinion, knocking is probably the most uncomfortable step in the process, but trust me, if you knock and listen you'll be on your way to becoming a miracle maker. If the backstories are unique and or at all similar, then you are ready for the next step of connecting with your mentee. Choose one of the three mentee recruits and move to the next step which is to connect.

The first part of connecting is making what I like to call "the ask." Now "the ask" is simple in a way, but important nevertheless. Once you knock, and the mentee recruit opens the door and begins to share their backstory with you, your next move is to connect by asking if it would be ok for you to mentor them for a specified amount of time. The ask does not need to come at the same time as the knock and please don't leave out the specified amount of time when making the connection. In other words, take some time before you ask to mentor someone and always consider the duration of your mentorship. If not, you'll hastily enter into a relationship and may give off the impression that you are committing to this role forever. Trust me, you may not be ready for that type of commitment right off the bat. As a rule of thumb, a good mentor relationship typically lasts anywhere from 6-12 months with you meeting with your mentee anywhere from 1-3 hours per month. You can spend this time doing whatever is necessary to make the relationship mutually beneficial. The bottom line here is to connect with your new mentee and already have the end in mind. Remember, mentorship is about

every moment, not just the overall process. I'll state this again;

consider the amount of time you are willing to spend with your

mentee before making the ask. If you're a veteran mentor, I'm

sure you get what I'm saying here. If you're a new mentor,

you're just going to have to trust me on this one. When you

make the ask let your mentee know why you chose them to

mentor. Make them feel like you have actually thought about

your relationship. It'll do wonders for the opening up of the

mentorship. Once you have made the ask now its time to

commit.

The final step in establishing a new mentor relationship

is committing to the relationship by receiving your new mentee.

We all have unique backstories, and it's almost never a fairytale

story. In fact, some people's backstory may be a little

unsettling, but as a mentor your responsibility is to look at your

mentee's past only as a reference and insight that you can use

to guide your mentorship. Before you can be cleared to embark

on your journey with your mentee, you need to fully receive
your mentee for who he or she is. Make every effort to not see
them in their current situation, but see them through the lens
of hope. A lens of expectation that your mentee's greater days
are ahead of them no matter what. Your mentee needs you for
a reason and now is a good time to get their expectations of the
mentor relationship. Find, Connect, Commit.

By now you are well aware of my idea on the miracle of
mentorship. And I hope you believe that there are miracles in
mentorship. Once you've found, connected, and committed to
your new mentee, you are now ready to embark on the journey
to uncover any number of hidden miracles from your
mentorship. As you embark on your mentorship journey, use
this book as a reference tool to help someone else become a
miracle maker. By reminding yourself about the power and
influence of mentorship you can become a *Miracle Maker.*

For now, I'm patiently continuing my own journey of
mentorship with my mentees and my mentors, and I know that

there are many more miracles to come. I hope this volume has given you inspiration to start, or continue mentoring somebody in this world.

#FindConnectCommit

You are a Miracle Maker!

My friend, you have made it to the end of this first volume of The Miracle Maker: Uncovering the Hidden Miracles in Mentorship. I hope that you have enjoyed reading my accounts of the miracles of mentorship in my life. Completing this project was an incredible process that has been in the making for a long time and now it is your time to to make miracles.

I'd love to hear about your stories on the miracles found in your mentorship experiences. **I have a challenge that I need your help with.** I want to compile a collection of 1,000 written accounts of miracles found in mentorship from all over the world. I want to feature your story in my next volume of The Miracle Maker. If you have a mentorship story that highlights a miracle—please share it with me on my website at **www.ericdcapehart.com**

The Miracle Maker

About the Author

Eric D. Capehart is a Professor in the College of Business at Tennessee State University. Eric is the Founder and President at All The King's Men, Inc.- A mentorship organization for males. He earned his BS in Speech Communications at Tennessee State University where he served as Senior Class Vice-President. Eric later earned a Masters Degree in Business Administration from the University of Phoenix and is currently pursuing a second Masters Degree in Professional Counseling at Liberty University.